LEVEL 2 READER

Junior's Lost Tooth

Based on the episode "Junior's Lost Tooth"
by Jorge Aguirre
Adapted by Gabrielle Reyes

Scholastic Inc.

Published by Scholastic Inc., *Publishers since 1920.* SCHOLASTIC and associated logos are trademarks and/or registered trademarks of Scholastic Inc.

The publisher does not have any control over and does not assume any responsibility for author or third-party websites or their content.

ISBN 978-1-338-86255-3

10 9 8 7 6 5 4 3 2 1   23 24 25 26 27

Printed in the U.S.A.   40

First printing 2023

Book design by Ashley Vargas

This is Alma and her family.
Alma lives with her parents,
her little brother, Junior, and her abuelo.
That's "grandfather" in Spanish.
Chacho is their dog!

1

Junior has some big news!

"Wake up, Alma!" he says. "My tooth is loose!"

"Wow! Your first loose tooth!" Alma says.

Junior is excited.
"I'm going to have a show when my tooth falls out. That way everyone can see it! My tooth will be a big star."

Junior runs to the kitchen.

"I have a loose tooth!" he tells his family.

"Let me see that wiggly tooth!" says Mami.

"The Tooth Fairy will visit you soon," says Papi.
"Then she'll leave you some money," says Abuelo.
Junior smiles. Then he gives everyone tickets.
"These are for my Tooth-tastic Show. When my
tooth falls out, it will be the star!"

Alma has an amazing idea.
"Let's go see Tía Gloria next door! Our aunt
will know how to get your tooth out!"

Tía Gloria has a plan.

"Junior, I have hot pepper pretzels. They are extra spicy. They are extra, extra crunchy! Take one bite, and your tooth will come right out!"

"Uh, no, thanks! Those pretzels smell too spicy," Junior says.
"I'll just keep wiggling my tooth."

Junior wiggles his tooth front to back.
He wiggles it side to side.
Pop! His tooth finally comes out!

"My tooth!" Junior shouts. "Now I can show it to everyone!"

"¡Wepa!" says Tía Gloria. "Nice work, Junior! Take a pretzel to celebrate."

Junior sniffs the hot pepper powder.
Ah . . . ah . . . Achoo!

Uh-oh! Junior dropped his tooth!

"Where did my tooth go?" Junior cries.

Tía Gloria looks under the rug.

12

Alma searches the couch.

"It's gone. I lost my loose tooth," Junior says.

"Now I can't have my Tooth-tastic Show."

"Junior is way, way, way sad. I wonder if
there's any way I can help?" Alma says.
She has an idea! "Be right back, Junior!"

"Junior, you don't need your tooth for the Tooth Fairy. I can give you tooth money!" Alma says.

15

Junior sighs, "Thanks, Alma . . ."
But he still looks sad.

Alma thinks. Then she runs to her room.
"I can give these to Junior. He loves
candy, comics, and dinosaurs."

"Here you go, Junior! Here are your favorite things. These will cheer you up!" But Junior still looks sad.

18

"Why is Junior so sad?" Alma asks.
"I gotta think about this."

"Junior was excited to lose a tooth. He wanted everyone to see it!"

"When it came out, he was so happy!"

20

"But he got really sad when he lost it."

"That's it! Junior really wanted to show everyone his tooth. I know what to do!"

Alma calls her family together.
"Everyone! We all need to look for
Junior's tooth!"
"Let's find it!" says Mami.

22

"Papi to the rescue!" says Papi.

"¡Vamos!" says Abuelo. "Let's go!"

Tía Gloria, Uncle Nestor, and Cousin Eddie
help too.

23

Everyone springs into action.
Uncle Nestor shouts, "I found it!"

But it's not the tooth.
It's his knight helmet.

Abuelo shouts, "I found it!"

But it's not the tooth.
It's his lucky sock.

"All this searching is making me hungry!" says Tía Gloria. "I need a hot pepper pretzel break."

26

She licks her lips and takes a sniff.
Suddenly . . .
Ah . . . ah . . . ah . . . Achoo!

Alma sees something go flying.

"Hey, look! It's Junior's tooth!" she shouts.

Plink!

"My tooth! I found it!" Junior says.

"Wow! It was in my hair!" Tía Gloria says with a laugh. "I really need a haircut!"

"You know what this means!" Alma tells her brother. "It's time for the Tooth-tastic Show!" Junior says, "Tickets! Tickets, please!"

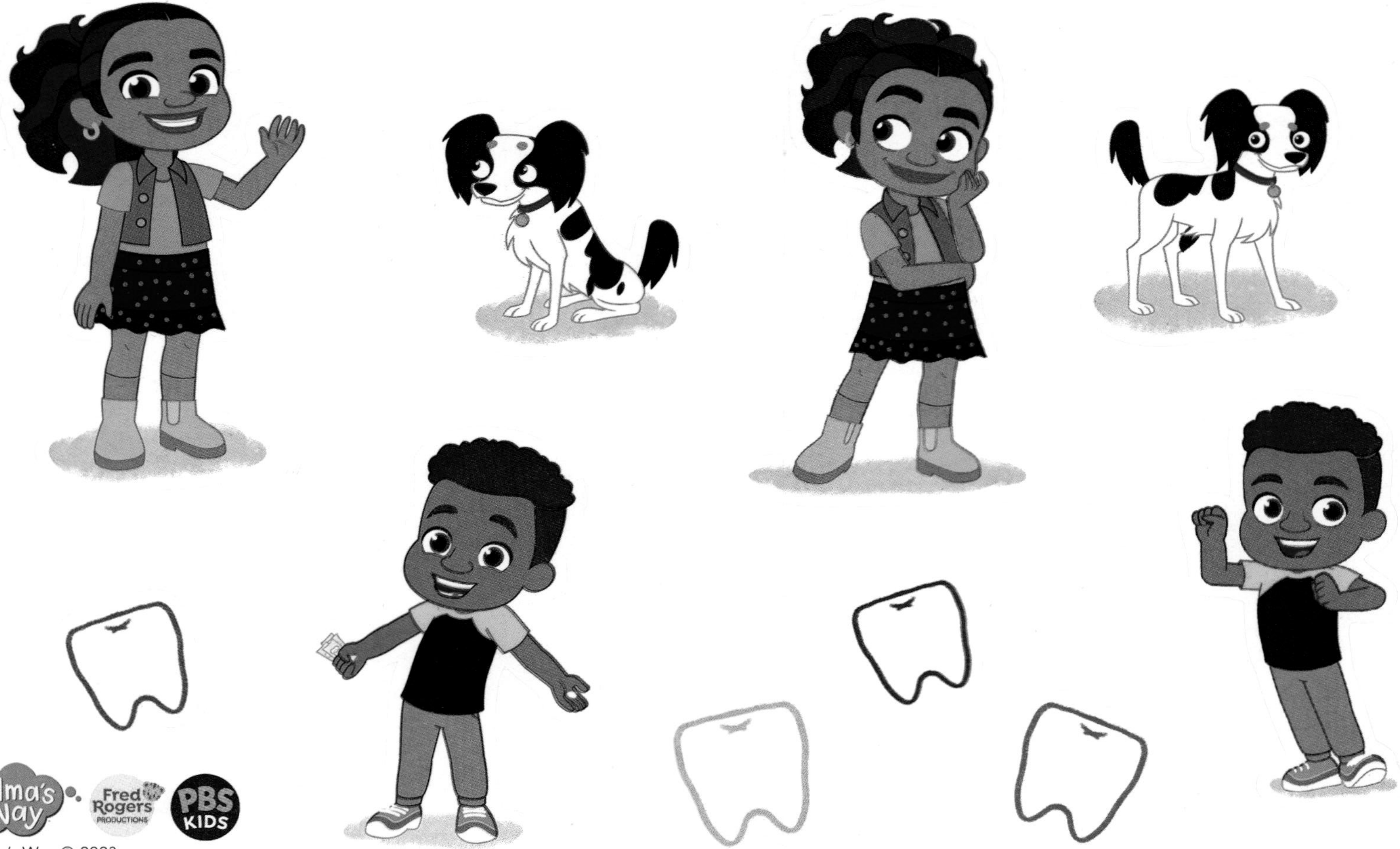